For my husband, John Conheeney, and his four youngest grandchildren,
Thomas and Liam Tarleton and John and Oliver Conheeney
With love
— M. H. C.

In memory of George R. Kaiser Jr. — artist, teacher, and sailor
— W. M.

⌐ ACKNOWLEDGEMENTS ⌐

Last year at a holiday signing, I was chatting with my longtime friend Wendell Minor, who illustrated four of my hardcover novels, including my first book, *Where Are the Children?*

His editors, Rubin Pfeffer and Paula Wiseman, were there and suggested Wendell and I collaborate on a children's book. *Ghost Ship* is the result of that conversation. Cheers and blessings to you, Rubin and Paula, for after making the suggestion, guiding us in the process of writing and illustrating this story.

Elizabeth Reynard's *The Narrow Land: Folk Chronicles of Old Cape Cod* and *The Mooncussers of Cape Cod*, by Henry C. Kittredge, gave me a great sense of life in the seventeenth century on my beloved Cape Cod.

I have so enjoyed going back in time to tell this tale and having Wendell Minor's exquisite illustrations to bring it to life.

– M. H. C.

A special thanks to Mary Higgins Clark for sharing her love and lore of Cape Cod, and to Rubin Pfeffer and Paula Wiseman for making this collaboration a joyous experience.

The illustrator also wishes to thank David Murdoch, of Chatham Water Tours, and the Chatham Historical Society for an in-depth perspective on the history and waters of Chatham, Massachusetts, and marine artist Mark Myers, whose illustrations in John Harland's *Seamanship in the Age of Sail* (Naval Institute Press, 1984) were extremely helpful.

Although *Ghost Ship* is a work of fiction, the illustrator has made every effort to infuse the paintings in this book with a sense of time and place.

– W. M.

SIMON AND SCHUSTER
First published in Great Britain in 2007 by Simon & Schuster UK Ltd
Africa House, 64-78 Kingsway, London WC2B 6AH
A CBS company
This paperback edition published in 2008

Originally published in 2007 by Simon & Schuster Books for Young Readers,
an imprint of Simon & Schuster Children's Publishing Division, New York

Text copyright © 2007 by Mary Higgins Clark. Illustrations copyright © 2007 by Wendell Minor
Book design by Wendell Minor. The text for this book is set in Edwardian Medium
The illustrations for this book are rendered with gouache watercolour

A CIP catalogue record for this book is available from the British Library

ISBN -10: 1-84738-087-5
ISBN -13: 978-1-84738-087-6

Printed in China
10 9 8 7 6 5 4 3 2 1

Ghost Ship
A CAPE COD STORY

MARY HIGGINS CLARK

Ghost Ship

A CAPE COD STORY

Illustrated by WENDELL MINOR

SIMON AND SCHUSTER

LONDON · NEW YORK · SYDNEY

Summer had begun and Thomas was visiting his grandmother who lived in a very old house in Cape Cod that had once belonged to a sea captain. Sometimes she told him stories about the great sailing ships that had come to Cape Cod many years ago from all over the world. She told him that in the old days when a storm suddenly began, a ship trying to reach harbour would be driven into the rocks and sand bars, where it would break up and sink.

Thomas loved to hear the stories. He wondered about the sea captain who had built this house more than two hundred years ago. He wondered if that sea captain ever lost a ship in a storm. He thought about that a lot.

One day Thomas went down the long flight of stairs from the lawn to the beach. He had promised his grandmother that he would not go too near the water until she joined him. His grandmother knew that Thomas would never break his word.

There had been a heavy storm the night before. The wind had whipped the waves until they slammed halfway up the stairs before crashing back onto the shore. Now the beach was littered with shells and rocks that had been washed in by the sea. Thomas began to sift sand through his fingers. The sand was damp, but he liked that.

Sometimes after a storm he would find unusual things that had been in the ocean. Once he had even found a small ring. His grandmother said it wasn't valuable but that it looked as though it had been in the ocean for a long, long time.

He wondered if after the big storm last night it was possible that he would find another ring. Or maybe he'd come upon an unbroken shell. If he did find one, he would put it up to his ear and listen, because shells hold the sound of the sea.

But then, suddenly, his fingers felt a hard metal object. He had to dig around it to set it free. It was much heavier than a shell. It looked very, very old. He ran his fingers over it and began to rub the sand and salt from it. But it was like trying to rub cement off a wall. He looked around and reached for a big rock and began to try to scrape the crust off whatever it was he was holding in his hand.

$\mathcal{A}$nd then something magical happened. The minute he managed to get down through the sand and salt, the metal object began to glisten, and the rest of the sand and salt got loose and slid away. "It's a belt buckle," Thomas exclaimed. "It's like the one I wore when I was a pilgrim in the Thanksgiving play at school."

*T*hou has found my belt buckle," a polite voice said. "I thank thee kindly. I lost it a very long time ago."

Thomas looked up. His eyes widened. He could not believe what he was seeing. Standing in front of him on the beach was a boy just about his own age.

Thomas blinked, not sure if he was dreaming yet sure that he couldn't be. He looked down and saw that the belt buckle was now so shiny that it might have been brand-new. It was carved with the picture of a ship, a ship that had four sails that billowed in the wind.

He knew he would give the buckle back, but first he wanted to talk to the boy. "My name is Thomas Fleming," he said. He pointed up to his grandmother's house.

"My grandmother lives there," he explained. Then because he wasn't sure what else to say, he explained, "Her house was built by a sea captain. His name was Andrew Hallett."

"My name is Silas Rich," the other boy explained. "I had the honour of serving Captain Hallett. He was a very brave man and truly a great seafarer. I was his cabin boy."

Thomas did not even bother to wonder why this boy who had lived so long ago was here. He just wanted to know about Captain Hallett and whether or not he had ever been in a shipwreck.

It was late afternoon and the lighthouse at Chatham could be seen blinking and blinking. Thomas knew it flashed twice every ten seconds. He pointed to it. "When Captain Hallett built this house in 1752, I know there was no lighthouse here and I know that many ships crashed coming into harbour. Did that ever happen to him?"

Silas sighed. He sat down cross-legged beside Thomas in the sand. "It was a disgraceful and shameful event," he said. "I truly dislike to call it to mind, but I can see thou admire the captain and I think it would please thee to hear the story. Captain Hallett was a very fine seaman and because of that some people were very jealous of him. He sailed the oceans with a sure hand. In his ship the *Monomoy* he weathered storms that would have sent other vessels to the bottom of the sea. In the year 1761 he had been away for nearly two years and was expected home. Word had come from smaller vessels that had met him nearing Boston Harbour that he was on his way. Everyone was in great hope for his safe return. He was a giant of a man."

Thomas could see the glow in the eyes of Silas Rich. He knew that he had not been wrong when he thought of Andrew Hallett as a hero.

"Tell me about him, Silas," Thomas urged. "You see, there is a portrait of him in my grandmother's house. It's out being cleaned now, but in it he looks so strong and so wise and so fearless. Was he really like that?"

$\mathcal{S}$ilas did not answer him directly. Instead he looked over in the direction of the lighthouse. "I love sober light," he said.

"Sober light? I don't know what that means," Thomas told him.

"Perhaps thou would say twilight . . . or . . . dusk. . . . What I mean is the time just before the sun is totally vanished in the sky. That was the way it was the night Captain Hallett returned from his long voyage. Then suddenly the wind whipped up. It does that, thou know'st."

Thomas moved around a little so that he could face Silas Rich directly. He could sense from the look on the face of his new friend that he was going to hear a story that had never been told before.

"My father had gone to sea before I was born. He never returned. But Captain Hallett was always very kind to me. He would take me out on his sloop . . . ," Silas began.

"Sloop?" Thomas asked.

"A small vessel. When he was home, he would go out on it and see to his grand ship, the *Monomoy*, when it was in harbour. My father had been his great friend and so I was, as he told me, forever dear to him. He promised me that when I reached my tenth birthday I would be appointed his cabin boy and sail with him."

Thomas was nine years old. He thought of what his mother would say if he asked to sail away and be gone for as long as two years.

$\mathcal{Y}$our mother would have let you go?" he asked.

Silas smiled. "She knew my father would have wanted me to go. She understood. The day was coming. Captain Hallett was on his way home and when he left again, I would be his cabin boy."

It had been a peaceful day after last night's storm. But then suddenly, as Silas spoke, the wind began to pick up. Thomas realized he was cold. He looked out at the water and saw how the white caps were higher and stronger.

"It was this sort of night in October when the captain was approaching harbour on the *Monomoy*," Silas said. "A Cape kind of storm came up, violent and without warning. Thomas, we had had a very dry time. The corn had burned in the ground before we could harvest it. The fields were parched. It was a rare and dreadful summer and autumn, and there was a great fear of fire. If a fire came, it could destroy our homes.

"And then one did break out miles away in Brewster Village. Word came that many houses were ablaze and the wind was driving the fire all through the mid-Cape. Aid was needed and at once."

"We have fires like that," Thomas said. "I live in California, and when the Santa Ana winds come, a fire may spread for miles."

Silas looked at him with a curious expression, and Thomas realized that he never would have heard of California or Santa Ana winds. "Did people go to fight the fire?" he asked.

"Every able-bodied man rushed onto his horse or hitched up his mule to his buggy and travelled to help. I wanted to go, but they would not allow anyone so young to accompany them. I started home most disconsolate and I am afraid quite downcast.

I knew I was strong and could be of great use passing buckets of water. But it was not to be."

Thomas was no longer aware of how chilly it had become. He wanted to hear the rest of the story.

"I had gone but a short distance when I heard the sound of a horse approaching. I stepped aside and observed that it was none other than Samuel Lewis, a sorry excuse for a man. I knew what he was up to. He had given the appearance of joining the firefighters and then when they rushed out of the village, had held his horse back, confident that in the confusion he would not be missed."

"He sounds like a coward," Thomas said.

"A coward he was and far worse than that. When he was captain of his own ship, he was a most careless mariner, and when a storm came up, his sails were shredded and his ship wallowed in the sand. Twenty-six brave sailors were drowned because of him.

y the time I reached home, the wind had become so harsh and cold that my mother sent me to fetch more logs for the fire. It was then that I saw a group of men sliding through the woods beyond our home. I wondered why they had not accompanied the other townsmen to assist in fighting the fire. Then I could see that they were carrying lanterns. Finally I was able to discern the face of the leader. It was Samuel Lewis. He was always jealous of Captain Hallett and I knew instantly what he was about. He had become a mooncusser and was planning to destroy the *Monomoy*."

"A mooncusser?" Thomas could tell from the way Silas said the word that it wasn't a good thing.

A mooncusser is a thieving man who would put lanterns on a beach to make the captain of an approaching ship believe he was in harbour. Then when the ship met shallow water and broke up, the cargo would wash up and the mooncusser would steal it."

Thomas just knew what Silas was about to tell him. "Samuel Lewis was jealous of Captain Hallett and was going to do that because he knew the captain was nearly home."

"Thou has grasped quickly his foul purpose, Thomas." Silas shook his head. "The townsmen were gone. Most of the women in the village had small babies and could never have left them. But I knew I had to save the *Monomoy* and could not do it alone."

Thomas thought about what he would have done if he had been watching the mooncussers setting off to destroy the ship. "There must have been other boys your age who were not allowed to go fight the fire," he said.

"Thou are very wise, Thomas. Yes, indeed, there were many children in every household, save of course for the elderly parishioners'. And so I ran to the nearest house and banged on the door of my friend Joshua and told him of the dreadful threat to Captain Hallett. He gathered up the logs in his backyard and his mother sent his small brother to alert our neighbours. Joshua and I dragged out logs to the beach, and then it was a miracle. One by one other lads our age were arriving and pushing and pulling their logs, the logs meant to keep their families warm, to the beach, this very beach, mind thee."

*W*here were the mooncussers and Samuel Lewis?"

"Perhaps a mile away, lighting their lanterns. We began our fire and flamed it higher and higher, but I still feared it would be too late."

"Captain Hallett would have seen the other lights first."

"Truly. I was in despair thinking how the captain had built his beautiful home and might never live to see it or his family again. And that was when I knew what I must do."

"Thomas, come up now." It was his grandmother calling him from the top of the stairs.

"What did you do, Silas?" Thomas asked. "I don't want to go until you tell me the rest of the story."

"Mistress Hallett had come out of the house and was standing on the top step."

"Yes . . ."

"I called to her to stand back. And I began to drag logs to the foot of the stairs. My friends understood what needed to be done and yanked and hauled the remaining logs to the stairs."

"You set the stairs on fire!" Thomas exclaimed.

"Yes, we did. We knew that they would flame high, and if the captain was nearby, he would see the silhouette of his home and know that he was not yet at harbour."

"Did it work?"

"It was just when the flames began to climb that one of our lads called out, 'He is there. I see the ship.'

$\mathcal{O}$h, Thomas, the brave captain was heading straight for the beach where the mooncussers were waiting. 'More logs, more logs!' I shouted. We tossed them on. We took off our shirts and threw them on the fire. The flames began to leap to the sky. Then just as it would have been too late, we saw the *Monomoy* change course. Oh, Thomas, the moment of glory and joy when we could discern that it set itself safely to harbour. And then like a gift from God, as he passed us and the still-blazing fire, the captain dipped his sail to give thanks to us. Later he told me that he could see his home bright sharp against the sky and knew that the course he was on would have brought him to doom."

homas," his grandmother called again.

"I am coming," he called back. "Oh, Silas, I'm glad I found your belt buckle."

"The captain gave it to me that night. For many years after that, I sailed with him. Later, after he retired and before I became a captain, I was in one shipwreck, but that was no one's fault. The Cape seas demand a return from the vessels that sail it. We all escaped safely, but in swimming to shore I had to remove my shoes and the buckle. I am most grateful to have the buckle with me now."

Thomas reached out his hand with the belt buckle. Silas accepted it and smiled. "Thomas, I thank thee. Thou are truly my friend." Then just as suddenly as he had come, he was gone.

$\mathcal{T}$homas hurried up the stairs. "I'm sorry, Gran," he said. "I know I kept you waiting."

His grandmother smiled. "I know you, Thomas. You were telling stories in your head. You're a dreamer, and it is a wonderful gift, to be a dreamer."

Thomas went into the house and was startled to see that the portrait of Captain Andrew Hallett was back over the fireplace.

"The restorer just returned it," his grandmother said. "Doesn't it look beautiful with all those rich colours that we couldn't see under the grime? And Thomas, see that beautiful belt buckle, the way it's carved with the sailing ship? Do you remember how, before it was cleaned, the buckle looked as though it was just a dirty piece of stone?"

"I remember," Thomas said. "I really do remember." *And I wasn't dreaming,* he told himself. *I know I wasn't.*